To Walter E. Peile

and all that you wait for!

Myra Cohn Livingston

I'M WAITING

MYRA COHN LIVINGSTON

I'm Waiting

WITH ILLUSTRATIONS BY ERIK BLEGVAD

HARCOURT, BRACE & WORLD, INC., NEW YORK

also by Myra Cohn Livingston

WHISPERS and Other Poems
WIDE AWAKE and Other Poems
I'M HIDING
SEE WHAT I FOUND
I TALK TO ELEPHANTS!
I'M NOT ME
HAPPY BIRTHDAY!
THE MOON AND A STAR and Other Poems

To Robert and Louis

on their first birthday

I'm waiting
    for the big circle sun
    to climb up the sky
    shining morning into my room.

I'm waiting
    for someone to come in
    and find me awake!
    Good-by, bed and pajamas!
    Hello, shoes and socks and clothes!

I'm waiting
    for my breakfast,
    cold juice and cereal, egg and milk.
    Hurry, toast. Pop up!

I'm waiting
  to run out into the morning,
  to take a tall ride into the swinging sky,
  to dig deep into the sandbox.

I'm waiting
   for a ride on my tricycle, far away,
   for a ball to roll, a wagon to pull,
   for a friend to come over and play with me.

I'm waiting
  to eat my lunch,
  soup and crackers, meat and cheese.
  What will be for dessert?

I'm waiting
    for a little nap,
    for my eyes to close, for sleep to come.
    The door shuts tight.

I'm waiting
    for my wake-up time.
    Hello, afternoon! Hello, toys!
    Where will we go today?

I'm waiting
for a ride in the car
to the park, the zoo, the grocery store,
and for someone to visit.

I'm waiting
    for supper sounds in the kitchen,
    for long cool shadows under trees,
    for Daddy to come home.

I'm waiting
    to jump in the big ocean of the bathtub,
    to be a swimming fish, a splashing frog,
    to climb over clean into my towel.

I'm waiting
for a last game,
for one more somersault and a book to read,
for someone to tuck me into bed.

I'm waiting
    for Mother's kiss and Daddy's smile,
    for a light burning in the hall,
    for my good-night prayer.